THE ANONYMOUS LOVER

THE ANONYMOUS LOVER

new poems

by

John Logan

Liveright New York

The author is grateful to the editors of the following
publications in which the poems in this book appeared:
American Poetry Review, Antaeus, Beyond the Square, Cafe Solo
Chelsea Review, Hudson Review, Iowa Review, Lillabulero,
Modern Poetry Studies, New York Quarterly, Panjandrum,
Rapport, Salmagundi, Mouth, Our Original Sins,
Southern Review (Australia), Toothpaste, Voyages.

Photographs on pp. 32, 35–6 courtesy of Aaron Siskind.

ISBN: 87140-084-7 (paper edition)
ISBN: 87140-564-4 (cloth edition)
Library of Congress Catalog Card Number: 72-97487
1.987654321

Designed by Mary M. Ahern
Manufactured in the United States of America

for my three daughters

CONTENTS

THE ANONYMOUS LOVER

In pools
along the wide terraces of shards of shale
shot
     with white
amid the rock colors of a lasting fall
there
        are
               these very gentle moves
of life—
             a wonderful solemnity:
see the secret algae,
mussels and the mottled dark
barnacles
that open up their mouths like baby birds
among the darting, delicate fleas of God.
At the edges of the sea's expanse
loom giant clouds of silent ships,
and just on
               beyond
                       the horizon
waits the little light-
ship I cannot quite
                  see.
But watch with me—
for soon it will show up
in this filtered picture that I snap.

Abstract Love Poem

All the heavy
          wet-
              ness
of the long rain
is held in deep green
spring grass
          gathering it
to capture all the light
which through ground
glass clouds
          has fail-
ed unmarked
          and now the sky is dull
more dark
          than
              the damp
                  green
but lighter than
the great trees that stand
immensely black
          cast-
ing in
     the green
          glow
of grass
     no
        shadow.

I hesitate
> to hurry up the path
disturbing the in-
> > timacies there
between
> green,
> > black,
the last
> light
> > and the moist air.

Riding on his bike
in the fall
or spring Fel-
lini-like twilight
or dawn, the boy
     is moved in some way
he does not understand.
A huge grey or green, long porched house
(he's partly color-blind)
crowns a low hill: rise-
s silent as a ship does
before him.
The vision makes him yearn
inside himself. It makes him mourn.
So he cries
   as he rides
     about the town.
He knows there are other great homes
and other beautiful streets
nearby. But they are not his.
He turns back.
    He gets off his bike
and picks
   up three fragments of unfinished pine
adrift on the green
     (or grey) lawn
thinking—hoping—that perhaps
there is something some place he can fix.

Well, Paul, when you were nine
I wanted to write
and now you're nearly twelve.
For too long I have shelved
this fact
      in an
         in-
accessible part
         of myself.
And the presence of it there
is like a blush
        of shame or
guilt inside the flesh
of my face. A fall
bloom of bril-
        liant gold about
to wilt
    beneath
obscure,
     heavy breath.
Your breath is sure
as the hearty new born
filling up your bronze horn
in the junior high band,
and your cheeks puff with it.
Your pockets bulge with hands
as you grin in the picture
about to speak
balancing on the side edges of your
            feet.

Poem for My Son

I have seen your new
beau-
    tiful
body dive
and dance one and a half times
into the pool.
My mind moves back
to where at nine I sat
in the bus on the big girl's lap.
And more than once
                  forgot my lunch
so the one ahead
            in the fourth grade
(believe
     it
       or not
named Glee!)
would give me sections of her
or-
   ange
not knowing it was all prearranged
inside
     my mysterious head.

2.

When I was young
I lived on a farm grandfather owned:
I remember in the cold
my small damp tongue

stuck on the hand-
              le of the pump.
My cousin Clark
and I got the calf to lick
us in the barn,
          but then
his father caught
            us and caught
us too smok-
ing big
    cigars behind the crib!
I carried cobs
         in buckets for the cook-
stove and cranked the separator hard.
Oh, I did
all my chores with a genial hatred.
Sometimes at night I lay
in waves
      of summer grass
feeling inside my chest
the *arching*
      of the search
          light *shin-*
ing from the distant town.

3.

When I was ten
         nobody said
what it was the dogs did
to each other, or the bull

(whom we never could
                  go near) and
the cow with the gentle bell.
                    The good
                    nuns told
me (I didn't ask)
that my dick
could only carry waste.
But they were wrong.
My son, you shouldn't have
to wait
        as long
as I to learn to love
and find for yourself
a bright, a sweet, calming wife.
There are some things not all fathers know
but if I could I would tell you how.

4.

Oh I remember times I wish
I could forget.
Once when the family took a trip
and stopped
           at a motel
you cried and cried.
We thought that you were ill.
Then at last you said
"Why did
        we have
               to move
to this small house?"

And the vacation time
when you got left behind
in the car while the other kids and I climbed
the mountain side.
When we came back you did not feel
well.
      You fiddled with the wheel.
My mind's eye
                goes blank as yours that day.
And once after the divorce,
confused, you asked in a small voice
(a mild one)
Daddy, do you have any children?
I do, Paul. *You* are one.

Chicago Scene
(for Roger Aplon)

At the bar called
                    Plugged
Nickel in Chicago
red, blue and yellow hammers
on its honky tonk piano
easily make their hits.
A boyish drummer ticks
his brush
              and pushes
back
      a shock
              of brown hair.
He draws lightly from his glass of beer.
A heavy scholar of the sax
mounts his giant bass
and together they begin
to snort,
              smoke,
                    and carry on
like a Saint George with dragon.
This certain beat
pulses to the puff of Bobby Connally's cheek.
And now the sweet and sour sauce
of the old New Orleans Jazz
potent as our father's jizz
permeates the air,

seems to knock us in the ear
and starts
      melancholy thoughts
(it is too loud to talk).
Behind the bar,
      oracular,
a bushy bearded (black)
and muscled man
      works
and broods. No one has ever seen
his face!
      For he's gone,
          proud,
to the dark side
      of the plugged moon.

Movies are badder
    than ever
in San Francisco.
Man, if you wish to go,
then perhaps you should listen
to what a midwestern
buff has to say:
They
  showed nude girls before
(crotch shots looming up near)
and, usually on alternate days,
they showed nude guys.
Next they let the naked fel-
low pretend to ball
(rather softly)
    the wildly
frenzied, faking girl.
But some of these
    amateurs could
not help taking their scenes
harder than they were told.
So now there's no pretense—
and, hence, this melancholy singing.
Frisco's dirty flicks are really into something!
Fucking, blowing, sixty-nine.
    And, *che sera*
      sera

let whatever comes, come.

Trouble is
       I'm not at all at ease
with the technicolored sur-
              facing of sperm,
sentimental music piped
          behind.
Trouble is
the patterning of pubic hairs
is not
    abstract.
Trouble is inside the cunt
I see more than a hint
of a human face
hooded, primitive, unfinished.
And there's a face in the head
of the erect
cock. A changing face rolls
in the balls
        as they make a further thrust.
Also a face at the breast
that will
      gather
round the eye or
the little
tough nose of the nipple.
There's another, more hairy face
in the man's chest.
Or in the back of the cares-
sing hand,
       the hollows of the thighs.

And
    always there is this
face
    in the *face*.
For our conscience views itself
in the mirror of the flesh.
Satur-
    day after-
        noon at the
movies. A far cry from the
Grande Theatre in Red Oak, Iowa.
Shit. With the porn
there's not even any popcorn.
So what should a boy from the Iowa farm
do when
    he finds himself in San
Francisco at a pornographic film?
Well, I guess
    he should just face the facts
and get his ass home.

(*after "The Anguish of Departure"*)

The two short,
                straight
bushes
        from deChirico's brushes
neither reach nor touch,
                        do not stretch.
Perhaps
        they are people?
Surely they are dwarfed,
are stalked by a forced,
rust red
        and
                naked
grotesque giant
                steeple.
(Chimney).
                Masculine sex
(that is)
        quite empty of mystery.
The gently roll-
                ing bell-
y and thighs
                I
see
   briefly
        land-
scaped in the background
                        behind.

The white
           clust-
                    er or cloud
which could
           be a sign
                    of hope
will not go up
over deChirico's building with its
three arches.
                    The arc of dreams is black
and streak-
           ed with grey as dead hair is
or as the dawn empty streets
of early March.
                    And even the arch
of despair's in shadow.
                    Ah, I know
that near arch of woman.
It's in the front by the foreshorten-
ed mathematic modern railroad car,
horse drawn,
           not brazen,
                    not far—
but iron wheeled to the ground in
the foreplay of the painting.
This arch of woman
                    more than
half-lit
      he left
(more than one might have wished)

quite unfinished:

          a poem cannot,

no, it *does* not

       want

          to utter

how eerily closed

         deChirico

kept the louvered shutters

over each of those

          three arches.

We all grieve behind them

in the anguish of departure—

each of us

      in his own

         anxious room.

Listen here,
              liver,
let's stop hurting me.
Okay?
I'm fed up with you
and your unsatisfied
demands
              for special foods
and highpowered drugs.
Don't you feel well?
I'm told you can't take pork or eggs,
and Carter's little pills
(our fathers' famous reds)
just aren't enough—
you want the hard stuff.
For my part
              I thought
we were once close
                      friends,
but you've become a dope
fiend,
        liver,
and made me your pusher.
Thus, I protest your changed
and your more ingrained
                      attitudes.
Like somebody writing ads
you've been giving me the hard sell.
I suppose I'll have to explain
if you've been listening at all
to my harangue:

"hard cell" is a pun. Well,
do you know that can lead to cirrhosis?
and don't you agree
     that would be
too much for the both of us?
I wish you'd consider
all the good times we've had together,
liver.
  Remember?
Please bear with me for awhile and
forgive me if I get mad.
I think you'll find I am dead right.
Which is preferable to being dead. Right?

II

First I'd like to try
     to pacify
you, liver,
    not just with a lecture
but with a poem—
and get you to heal up your xylem
and phloem.
     Oh, I'm
aware those are parts
     of plants
(I was a biology major)—
but I speak in a circulatory metaphor.

Or, similarly,

       I might have used a simile,

which is a word like "smile."

But again I'll

have to expand what I mean

for, obviously,

          considering pain,

you know little about poetry.

Get this for one thing:

"Poets like

      to drink."

But then you invoke

Your damned Victorian ethic

and I hear the reply:

"you do something I don't like

and just wait—

I'll make you smart!"

It seems the philosophy

of your physiology

          is in an infantile

stage still.

May I point out this then:

an infant never wrote a poem.

Really, liver,

      why not

just admit

      you're an ig-

norant and selfish boor.

You have to have what you desire

or things get rough.

Before long you just want to go off
into the wild blue yonder
and take me with you.
Well, no
      wonder,
my poor, pining liver.
For you and I have been lovers:
I mean we really cared.
Now, truth is, you've got me scared.

III

Liver,
      I know that
you and I are stuck
in this thing together
and we're alive—
but if you are such a fart
that you insist
      on hurt-
ing me,
      then I say
I want out
      of this
        relationship.
I want a divorce
(get back into circulation).
Don't you read the newspaper,
        liver?
Find out what's happening in the nation?

Have you ever really faced
the fact that you can be replaced?
I tell you this domestic hassle
is not for me. I'm bored.
I say it's for the birds.
Gaggles of geese or vultures.
So, get off my back,
                liver!
Or at least stop peck-
ing at me.
Who do you think
              you are. Zeus?
Well, I'm not Prometheus.
Fact is
       I have a reverse
              Prometheus complex.
For instead of stealing fire
             I lose it.
"Give me some light!"
(Claudius to Hamlet).
or "Mehr Licht," as Goethe said
when he died
        shut in
           behind a curtain.
Or contemplate
        the sense of that
phrase
    the Ancients use:
"liver and lights."
But . . . I'm afraid I'm not getting through:

you
     just can't see
poetry.
          Well let's simply look at
some biological, even financial, facts:
Did you know that if you stay longer
you accumulate more gold, liver?
the richest source of Vitamin A ever discovered
was the liver of a snake (python)
estimated to be a hundred years old
when it died
                    in a zoo in London.
And the halibut liver
                         is richer
than cod, as scientists hint,
because cod is a mere adolescent
at the time of the sale of it
as contrasted with the older halibut.
Oh, to hell with it—
the lecture
               won't work either.
I'll tell you where you're at,
liver, you're illiterate.
But, after all, you're as old as I am—
Why, as it seems,
must I "come back to tell
                         you all?"
Thank God you know me at least
as well
          as any body.
So why give me such a bad time?

Did you forget your very name
signifies
   that which lives, not dies?
For Christ's sake, liver,
what are you, an Indian giver?
Why don't you just cut it out? Stop
complaining and do your job?
Are you so choked with bile
that despite
   my obvious fondness
you look on all my proposals with jaundice?
Or do you just like to hear me rave?
Still, I feel our relationship
     can be saved.
I don't want to say "this is it."
You can understand that.
Now, I hope you feel ashamed.
I hope you change your ways.

IV

You'd better!
Because when I took
you down to the doctor
he clucked
  (as you pecked)
and said you were growing larger.
Now, when a doctor says that to a kid
he usually pats him on the head.

The Doc
        did not
                pat
                        you—in fact
he pounded you a bit.
Liver, what the hell do you think you are?
Just a growing boy? Jesus—
perhaps you're going into your oedipal phase
and that's why you're so mean.
You're getting just too big for your britches.
That's
        why you hurt
                    and have these itches.
You know if you were
                        the liver of a polar bear
bounding
        down
some glacial hill,
they say you could
contain enough vitamin to kill!
At any rate
           you've got
too large for what the docs call
your "capsule."
But, with me,
it's not just that
old cop
(out)
        attitude—
                that you have to be stopped

and slapped
          back into your cage
(rib).
       That would be just too glib:
The *sad* thing is you've begun to change
                        my image.
For when I heard you were getting bigger
I looked at myself naked in the mirror,
and it's to you alone I have now confided
the fact that I appear lopsided.
I mean to say
you have ruined my symmetry!
Destroyed my manly beauty.
Because of your increased heft
my right side is twice as big as my left!
And you've made me a freak!
So, in conclusion, I say fuck
you, liver.
Do you think my heart is going to grow larger?
Or that this will affect
brain, glands, neck?
Stomach, balls and cock?
God, I'd be like that ten foot
                    fake
Fourth Century Etruscan warrior at The Met.
You've Oedipus-wrecked me
both horizontally and vertically!

V

Wait, I'm raving again
(Dionysius without gin):
And now it's me who feels ashamed.
What I really want to remind
you is this: the side
you're supposed to be on
                                 is *mine*.
For side is not a physical
concept. It's spiritual.
I think
          this confusion becomes habitual
whether or not we drink.
And like a dark mirror
                               this reflection, liver,
brings me to self-recognition:
For I have to be on your side
too: I have also hurt
                                 you
and injured *your* image
with a passion very much like rage
(of which you are the seat).
I can see it makes sense
it was the angry liver angry Zeus
attacked.
              Prometheus
                               is shackled
like a goose that's gorged
with corn to enlarge
its gland for the special feast.

That goose's feet
are nailed to a wooden floor
spiked through the poor
fragile webs
like the bird of the Christ Fable
prepared on the giant table
of the cross, whose crumbs, whose dregs
of wine the priests and poets drain:
they munch the body of the young bearded
man
     (thirty-three) who hangs suspended
over the twelve men banqueting
in Dali's painting:
                  robes stripped from him
he has hair beneath his arms
                      that are
spread-eagled in the clear air
of truth.
         For thirty days the goose's
liver grows, force fed.
And perhaps three days later that bird
with his pried open mouth and throat
is like us, twice dead.
I say let's decide
               instead
to be twice alive.
I want to open (willingly) the mouth
of my youth
        and breathe musical breath into it.

VI

Therefore
let's stop this war
within the body politic,
a conflict
neither of us can win.
I want to atone,
and speaking less
as angry father to a son
(or the reverse)—
and more like a priest
                        or brother
say, "Let's cease.
Let's forgive each other."
                        Finally
in my lecture, sermon, letter, poem
(which, like you has grown over-long)
I speak for the poets and the mothers,
                        as one of them
and simply plead, "let it be born
for the time has come:
let my belly return
flat as a man's belly again
so that at least for here
and now (perhaps for ever
if God is no deceiver)
you and I
                may be
our own
                deliverer."

I.   The louvered lids
of the still lived-in, hard
Roman House behind
(its old household heroes whole
a bit longer
        in the shelter
of their niche along the inner wall)
are heavily shut
        against
the sad, weathered stone
of the father and his shadow son,
whose curled head and torso have already gone.
The father's eyes still stare at God,
and his face is furious with hope.
His shattered arm once gestured
to protect
        his beloved son, now dead.
The father's still alive although the pocks
of time deepen and grow black
along his rock thighs, and time
too has broken down
his jaunty Roman prick.
But the stony hair remains
upon his belly and his son's—
like moss or winter wheat
as from the north of Rome
weaving from the graves of the brain.

II.   Into the wet, brief,

                        green and white
flash of weeds
your ancient stone shade now leans
at dusk
sick as a melancholy youth,
the blind too-smooth face
stained
with moss and memory both,
the strong, graceful feet first
taking on the color of the earth.
This ghost seems never to have had a nose.
Yet it has the bearing of a once
beautifully formed man:
Roman student, soldier, citizen,
toga carried back proudly
from the perfect, nude body
and hung loose from the young shoulder.
Now the flesh has gone slack from weather,
the face and loins made flat
by the terrible wedge
of a very slow sculptor,
and muscles of the back and legs
copied in an athletic prime
are made old and impotent by time.
A thousand and a thousand years since you are gone,
and then the long decay and death *of the stone.*
Must your face again go blank in a poem?

III. I could not decide

                    in this either hot or iced
weather
      or both (of the heart) whether
you stare wide-
eyed with fear,
             surprise,
                  or shock.
Sure it's a surprise
this leading so many lives
when you thought
             you'd chosen
one of them,
        not
           two or more
or
  none of the above—i.e., tried
suicide.
      So I eyed
your nose
        again but could not recognize
whether it was aquiline
(as
  my brother, that tease,
used to say of mine)
or smooth, since,
            as if by some contin-
uing token, your
          stone
           nose
is broken.

The unfinished poem
moves to your mouth, sensual as a ripe,
thick-veined scarlet
                    fruit,
                              pert,
or finally
            just surly.
                        And is your
long, marble hair
                    a boy's or a girl's?
It is the two curled
                    lines—
one bright,
            greater,
and one smaller—
pouring out of your
                    mouth rather
                                than in
which seem
            to sum
                    or sym-
bolize
        what stone,
                    camera,
and poem try:
for these streams of water
gather
        back again
                    in
your teeming, unbroken basin.

The beautiful, bodiced

                       yellow dress you had
and your long

              brown hair in the late
spring

       your eyes glint-
ing with wet

            that was not tears
(it

  was the moisture
of ferns,

       their
young, light haired fronds
unwind-

       ing, bending in the wind
together).   So it began.
We walked, we two, married (just)
In the Iowa City street

                quite aware
of our

      rings

         whose new gold, glancing
in the sun, seemed to make the finger

  lighter:

       we hoped
they'd be seen by others.

We climbed on the bus and sat side
by side
       weaving
our hands together, reaching
for the feel of each
other
       through the small but fierce
intervening flesh.
Off the bus
       we walked on, and we wished.
Long, almost silent walk,
the always whoring or always virgin
sun
     blazing blue, gold, orange as it dropped:
and the long, inarticulated wish
like a many-toned print or water color wash
yearning, anxious, strange—
the eternally ancient
              (yet
in some sense young) hope for change.

II

Just as the light
       began to be lost
we walked beside
       a freshly growing field,
and then at once turned
together as we heard

a very gentle, shuffling sound
with
     an unmistakeable feeling of breath.
A breathing.
        Huge, dark figures were quiet-
ly moving
      through a gate
and spreading themselves still and
great through the field.
Some of them bent
       ghostly, beaut-
iful, to brush along the ground
with their long, lean heads.
Some few stood alone quite
         self-possessed
in the failing light
       and others stretched
themselves to touch.
       The gate closed
as the last colt
      lurched
slightly drunk or mad or wild
through the soft, half-light.
Then the groups simply stopped
moving
     and were caught
it seemed
    in a steaming
or fogged, fleshed and powerful tableau

in the twilight's
                  thickly purpled glow.
The meadow
        now
             dark and filled
(I should
        say the fulfilled
field)
      blend-
            ed itself with each of them
as we walked away
             along the shadowy
disappearing fence

III

to our first house,
           Home.
The honeymoon room.
               Structure now gone—
with my records, an
           un-
gainly four-legged phonograph
               with doors, height
and all that
        (a kind
           of absurd shrine)
and my books:
          a second floor
              bay window

with a chair
   from which the libido
       floats, looks);
heavy tapestried, linen
     curtain
       on
the wall behind
    a candled
     altar,
for we were
   religious then.
And a bed.
    I took off my shoes
       and wiggled my toes
lying on the floor in that first room
excited by them
    (toes I mean)
       and fascinated,
flabbergasted
    by you—warmed
together by the presents of our friends
     around us
       in our new house.
Shy, we
   undressed separately
you in our room
    I in the bath down
the hall. "My god,"
    I said

to myself (not quite pajama clad),
"This is exciting as hell."
The knowledge that my hard-on
                                        would soon
have another use
                        than in the past
(terribly tired of loving a fist)
made
            me paradoxically calm. And glad.

IV

I must tell something more
                                    of her.
For she gave up much to be with me:
School (She was a junior
when I met her),
brief affair with another lover. Family.
Her
        brown hair
                        is long as I have said,
and that yellow dress she made
herself; besides she was very good
at seeing what is real and necessary—
a kind of
                anguished god-
                                    dess at managing money.
She
        had the nearly haughty
look and bearing of aristocracy.

To tell the truth her
               hauteur
half turned
         me on.
Invited to the Caribbean
by her father
            in the summer
she chose my own
               less colorful, slowly drain-
ing ocean.
        The profile line
of her neck and face
had a Pollaiuolo portrait's grace.
And the aura of her presence and her talk
brought meaning, memory and hope
                      back.

V

I was a virgin
         when
we went to bed.
           (Not that this
is
  so unique or sacred.
All of us were virgin once.
And many spend years along the fence.)
Oh, I know words cannot catch
much
      of the experience of sex.

On the other hand
painting, sculpture and music can—
the first two because we see or even
feel the textured flesh through them;
music because music's sound
like time
            moves behind, together with, or runs ahead
of spirit and mind.
It was the tenderness of meeting
that surprised me. Going
from my known man's land
into the flowering country of woman.
Part of myself moving inside you gently or thrusting, kicking like an unborn child
in its development.
Or like a live fish of silver or gold
now darting, now suspended quietly,
in your rich, profound, uncharted sea.
And you—you danced with me,
sometimes led
                sometimes followed.
I knew what loving meant
and for the first
time pointed myself toward your woman's heart—
tried to touch it with my groping, masculine hand,
as I felt you grip
                    me
                        and ungrip me
with your closing and opening body.

You and I felt
        that we were lost
                (or for a time spurned)
parts of each other now perfectly returned.
Predictably,
        I suppose,
             we
came too soon
        that honeymoon time
and shrank
      back
        into our own tight skins.

VI

The great, bright, moon shaped crab creature
rests, having just crawled up on the shore.
Land leans away from the sea.
A giant cloud, changing shape, leaves the sky
black or blue or grey.
The crimson crowned, great eyed king is dead,
but long live his shriveled child!
Every troubled, dreaming young man
lets go the girl in his hand.
And the tired parents of each of us
turn over to sleep at last.

My hand clicked on
                    the dead man's
                              lamp.
Its hanged crystals weak-
                    ly rang
(did not weep)
                    out of shape
under its shroud of dust which
covers too the plastic
fern and fake, foolish rose.
If those
        live
spirited lilies
                one sometimes sees
are real presents for the dead,
then what weird grave
                          could these flowers deck?
I'd guess
        the tomb
                (his or mine?)
of him who took sick
                    and died
never having been alive.
Here I still stay
and look
        at (soak up)
His relic stuff.
                His books—
one's a not
so NEW DICTIONARY (1928).

And one of them's in
                    Ovid's Latin.
And there's an ENCYCLOPEDIA OF THE WORLD
beside
        a cardboard
mounted photo of mother and child.
A milk glass wedding jar
                        for
the nuts and candy he once ate,
mouth and eyes turning more
and more
            out of the light.
I sleep
        in his bed trembling with chill
while the little rolls
                    of lint shed
or blow together again
along the ashen, old
brocade-papered wall.
On one dresser laid out
                    neat
the dead man's
ball point pen.
In the same line,
a tiny, brass
            ceramic box (to keep his stamps in,
although the letters all
                    are mailed),
scissors, screw driver, and file
for his finger nails (they'll still
grow for a little while.)

There's a darkening,
                    rather heavy chain
with a silver dollar (1896)
for the keys, now laid separate
and flat,
          that fit
the dead locks.
And in another line's
                    his magnifying glass,
aluminum flashlight case
(batteries yanked out safe
and lined up or ranked); retractable measuring tape
snapped back from the length of his life;
pocket knife, machine file and an awl,
some used and unused screws and nails,
paper clips for his uncompleted works.
At the side a still
elegant sil-
          ver comb and brush.
A cache of drugs
drying, such as cough drops,
and some wash
                    for the dead man's mouth.
Tie pins wait, one plain, one pearl
and the garish ties of which he was fond
(I mean the ones that do not bind)
line up limp along the wall
beneath a rack of family plates
recording souvenir sights.

A bit far-out
             the pictures on the opposite wall:
A luscious Renaissance girl
nude, leered at by her
                  elders—
and a photo of a classic sculpture,
a naked youth
              lean muscled arm upright
pulls his sword out of the throat
of the enemy (or friend) he quarreled with.
The sampler with its embroidered carriage—
its colorful Victorian couple who hope or hoped
once for marriage
                and its message:
"All to myself I think of you
"Think of the things we used to do.
"Sometimes I sigh, sometimes I smile
"But I keep each olden, golden while
"All to myself."
And on a shelf
             this lonely dead man's
framed
       himself
from far back as his own youth:
in undershorts, muscles soaking sun
being just as alive as the young body can.
Here are the clothes
              he throws
off: shoes
          someone shined and gave trees

to: a pair of pants
lying formless as a ghost
with the pockets all turned out
(offwhite like the balls of eyes)
and a still dirt-
                    y, red woolen shirt
which has already lost
                    its human smell.
His tables, candles, clock and bowl.
His mirror
          losing silver,
where now, this day I stand
                    and
suddenly am afraid!
For my god I see in the glass—
only the contoured back
                    of my own head!
And here, here is the bed
where I have lain these three nights past
and felt the mirroring pillow fit
closer and closer to his
the hollows of my own face.

I
(*for my daughter*)

This red
          Italian hand
blown glass
               vase
narrow as the very young
stem
     of your age,
Theresa, has a flame
shaped
          flaw
white
     as the stark
movement in
               my scarlet brain
when
     I think forever
(like a curse deliver-
               ed *to* me)
of the fire screaming in the Christmas tree
New Year's Day night
you fled tall
               with your beautiful
fire
     colored hair
(your face white

even in the heat)
into the flaw-
       ed snow
with its wrong
       red tongues.

II
(*for Phyllis*)

At my best I'll
                drive
around
        that island
just with you again and
wade
        in the glinting warm
Hawaiian
                waves,
put my hand
around your nicely naked waist
as it shimmers with wet
about the islands of your breasts
and drink champagne
letting it spill
                and surf a little
on my chin
when I'm
startled by your living face
beside me suddenly at the beach cafe.

We all live
               on islands.
And you and I've
                   wand-
ered far this day
on one: on Maui
enroute
          to Hawaii
which they call
                 the Big Isle.
I've gone farther than you have
because I find myself
catapulting away
from you as if afraid
                      to meet,
then back.
                Though it is
a horizontal zig
                  zag,
I thought
          of the vertical drop
of young men,
                 a rope of hemp
around their feet
in the initiation ceremony
down a sheer hill
that (without skill)
could easily crack the skull.

We've seen the beautiful
pink
anthurium plant,
part of it
erect out of its broad
adamic leaf, the scarlet I'iwi
bird
and the strange-boned
gorgeously formed
and mixed
native girls with hibiscus
in their dark hair.
That far
sheer, ancient wind-blown
mountain,
lush
at its base,
its long
feminine
erotic lines
partly shrouded
hushed
in mist,
the sun sometimes just
catch-
ing for a moment
the rocketing red
ohi'a-lehua flowers
which spring up
in the wake

of volcanic fires,
the yellow mamani
clustered like a family
                    of friends
on their stalks in bril-
                    liant patches
along hills
        and roads above
the native
            houses
or the falling terraces
                    of taro fields that
run
    stretching down
                    like quilts
or tawny animal pelts
toward the sea again.

II.

You are patient with the pain
I keep
        which I can
neither explain
                (even to myself)
nor escape. And therefore I half
begin
        to love you, as your
quick black hair

lifts as gentle
                    as your brown eyes still
seem
        in the wind
that shifts from higher up the sacred ground.
At Pihana you stand
                        where Kamehemeha shed
the blood of young Hawaiian men
in thankful sac-
                    rifice
some few of his bat-
                        tles won. (He was
turned on to blood
                        by Captain Cook—
who was torn apart—
and he showed
                a tenacity like
that of the later ministers
                        of Christ.)
The stones of the *heiau*

                    now
are the horrid black
                    of that
old
    dried blood.
Once before, you said,
                    you took
three
    of these
holy stones away
                and they've

caused you more cursed grief
than
    you deserve, Peter, my friend,
well-meaning thief.
But there's just
       too much
          dangerous life
in these ghosts they've left behind.
Perhaps
    the sensual red Af-
rican torch ginger
should first have made you wonder.
For my part
I
  wonder if the urge to rape
an orphan child
      and steal
his semen,
     leaving his bones all
broken up
     and black
inside the private temple of his flesh
is like that sacrifice
by which Kamehemeha thieved
young life
    for himself
and for the wife-
      ly earth into which
it still soaks
    slowly back.

It
drips
in the enormous mother vein
or extended island cunt
left by lava tubes
         we found
and went
       through
           underground.
Kamehemeha had less *mana* than
               his son,
you said,
     my guide,
        and less even
than his queen
whom he therefore needed
          to approach naked
on his belly
      like a baby.
A thousand youths he threw
(or like a mad Circean swineherd drove)
over
    the Pali,
       Oahu cliff
of sheer
     fall and of
sure,
    overwhelming beauty—
where the wind's so strong
it sometimes
      hangs

you or wafts you back again
like a sorcerer's wand,
or like the spores of ferns
or the cork-
           like
seeds of screw-pine
the waves will float
                  for months.
My own seas, my winds,
are weak today
           and I
depend
        utterly on you,
who do not know,
              so now
you walk
        suddenly out of my sight
if only for a minute
and I begin
        to trem-
ble with the panic of it.
My eyes drop at once
from this beautiful island place
to my own two feet
which I see
        monstrous
in their blackened socks
              split
by plastic thongs
into two club shaped parts

like the frozen lava flows
from Haleakala.
The naked feet of Hawaiian
men
    and women
are graceful as their hands.
But my feet
are black and swollen
because I've died in this exotic heat
that gives
        life
to all other manner of men,
               women and plants,
the hanging red
        Heliconia, the hundred orchid kinds,
and Tamarind.

III.

Peter, my absent
        friend,
the blood of boys, flowering,
may keep
    an aging king
alive, but not me.
I should have healed
        my grotesque feet
in the silver pool
in the valley of Iao

at the green root
of its great
          rising, aged pinnacle.
But I did not.
And now again, it's too late.
For Christ's sake
                    Peter why don't you come back!
If you're really gone for good
would
          you at least
                    respect my wish?
On my Maui grave
I want someone to leave
a half-
          empty bottle of wine
(perhaps some food
                    for our continuing need.)
And don't let
          some kid
steal it from my tomb!
Just give me that
                    blood-red funeral urn
at my foot. Perhaps an uwekahuna, wailing priest,
may wander by then
                    toward home
and in the trained, spirited light
from his lean body
you will all see
the gorgeous white plumeria trees
that fill
          my cemetery up like girls.

IV.

Thank
    God
        or Madam Pele
whose fiery
          goddess home has been on Maui
and is now in the still smoking
sometimes flowing
young Volcano where we head—
the desolation blasted stretch
on Hawaii.
         Or thank someone I say—
even Apua'a
        the lusty pig
god whose prick
        is like
a cork
   screw.
Thank one of them that you
are walking back in sight again.
I know you've been
         looking for green leaves
to place on
     the stones
        of the heiau
in hope of a safe passage
          for all of us.
But please don't
     go
again, Peter.

(That's my oracular

message.)

Don't leave,

and don't let me drive,

but get me out

of this astonishingly bloody place

and after this

please keep such terrible beauty to yourself.

Note: "Haleakala" is a dormant volcano on Maui.
"Heiau" and *mana* are Hawaiian for "sacred place"
and "sacred power" respectively.

The morning
   island light begins
to grow
   and now
the cocks cry
   at giving birth
to the colors
   of our day.
Their feathers make the dawn
blue and red and green
and they will strongly brighten up their combs,
as in the cold lodges
our women drop
naked to their haunches
      pok-
ing at the tepid fires.
Why, they will go out bare
to bring in another log
before coming back to bed!
The flames they build
as they squat
   and hug their chilling breasts
form halos in their pubic hair
      for
they are hunched in the ancient shape
of hope.

The fire place
with
its fine wisps
of smoke
suddenly fills with peace
opening like
the great, God-wide
canyons of Kauai
that drop clean from the clouds into the sea,
their distant threads of waterfall
like darts of light playing on the wall
and on the
body.
The woman will give us what she can.
We men will take what we are able.
(Painted blue
the Sibyl
inside ourselves is also writhing there—
some kind of dance about the same, uncertain fire—
I do not know what for).
These early women, wives, lovers,
leave their dawning chores
and coming back needing to be held
will hold
us too.
They already see
we do not know our fathers
and cannot learn to love our brothers.
But they will do what they can
once again

to warm our gut
                    and heart
and also that secret, incomparable cold
that grows upward from the groin
when we learn
                    we can lose a son.

The surfers beautiful as men
                                        can be
ride the warm
                        blue green
                                        swells
and the white sand is alive with girls.
Outriggers (double boats) ride the waves back in
as the native warriors did.
I tried to swim and tried to look,
but ended up just going back:
a huge, perfect black
man at the beach
somehow drove me away a block
to St. Augustine's Church.
The bodies were giv-
                                        ing me a fit
and I have come to seek the momentary calm
we find sometimes in the musk of Christ
(when he was awake
                                        and sweat-
ing blood
                as others slept,
or like a furious bouncer
hustling out the money changers.)
The bodies of Mary and Christ
both still live, we're told. They're alive
and thus
must have dealt with the stress

of that long time
                    of turning on
to being young.
I speak of teens.
                    Fifteen and ten
years ago when I first confessed,
it was in this same church built then
as a gigantic shed
where the strange Hawaiian birds
(I forgot their names—no matter)
flew in and out of the high wood-
en rafters
like the whimsical winds of grace,
and grace gives back to sight
what beauty is—
                    as
that loveliness at the beach.
Now the church
                    has been rebuilt
in pointed stone across the street
from a much
                    higher new hotel
where at lunch
                    I almost spilled
and found I could not eat
the purple orchid in my drink.

Along the back farm road the
Jacaranda
                and (still on Maui) the
Bougainvillea
burst like purple bushes struck with fire,
polyps burning under water.
                                        And far below
the unutterably blue
"Sea
        of Peace"
bare-
        ly shows itself, a more
ancient symbol
even than the Paia Montokiji Buddhist
temple
                we just passed,
where a few
                        chanting women sew.
Above us the
                        fecund rain forest
and the weird loveliness
of the bright orange illness
on the grey Eucalyptus tree's
flak-
        ing bark,
whose fragrance fills
the twilight
with its bittersweet
                        oils.

We walk together
                out of our
human love
I don't mean walk *out* of
it, but
        within. Still we are more separate
than either of us might
wish at the depths of our lives,
and we leave our friends
                        behind
in the car,
            their
lives and limbs entwined
like the roots of trees
apparently
            beautiful as the name of
that one: Macadamia.
Or Avocado.
And the slow,
grey sheep whose coats begin to glow
in the going light,
their faces start-
                ling black
as they make
their yearning, childlike
                    music;
and the yet
            blacker cows with faces white
as mimes
        amble up
                to us

pleased with the grass
                    we pull
from beside the road
and toss
into their field; in their shud-
                              dering ancient peace
these cows and sheep
quietly take their fill.
I feel
It is our love that must
                         just
nibble at the exotic hill.
There is a white
upper
        half-flower
where we walk
(whose bloom is now growing dark),
the Naupaka of the Hill.
The Naupaka of the Sea turns its other half-circle
of lower petals
from the dis-
                    tant Pacific
this
      way.
Is it because of me
we both seem Naupakas of the Hill?
Or is it because of imperfect
                              human love it-
self
      we
seem two Naupakas of the Sea?

The fog
            stammers everywhere
along the rock
                  break-
water pier
               and in the twilight air
the Peace
Bridge has its Buffalo steel feet
nearly all cut off.
                    Therefore it walks
like a lame centipede quite
impotent at first
then on to
            Canada.
Fishermen
            are chattering in
the fog.
        It's not
just the sign of them on the shore
I hear
but also the live laughter
of those boys with their poles
moving toward us,
breaking through the holes in the mist
which then again will fill.
I turn to you.
                The two
of us hunt
            for shells

(which somehow in or through their in-
tricacy have
                managed to stay alive),
and for the April plants—
Here alone the predictable, unruly grass
sprouts again and mounts
these unlike-
                ly rocks
where the ice has only just
                                broken up
again. I fix my
                hand
about your rich, young body,
your light ass.
                As we are about to kiss,
your small daughter who has run ahead
grows afraid
in the suddenly lost
                light.
She screams and tosses
                                up
toward the gathering thin
                                moon
the dead,
        admired fish she held
in each of her hands.

(*In Memoriam: Eric Barker*)

I

Peering, stung,
              bleared, hung-
over and lame,
through the waves of spray,
I feel somewhat
              panicky,
weird, about my sweat-
                    ing body.
For where do we and our vapors end?
Where does the bath begin?

Strange to be able to see through the steam
(but satisfying, to the point of calm,
like the vision of the perfect, new born)
for the first time
the whole,
              beautiful body of a friend.

Like a god
              damned eternal thief
of heat,

clouds
wreathing round
your black, bearded head,
belly, limbs and your sex
(but no piercing eagle about,
yet)
you lie flat on your back
on the rock
       ledge bench in the bath,
Promethean in your black
         wrath.

II

In our nun's or monk's
       black
rubber hoods
(lace-paper coifs
       just visible at the tops
of our heads),
as if about to pray,
and black rubber coats
       to our feet
because of the spray,
we walk the Niagara Tunnel.
You can tell
       almost for sure
which ones the kids are,

but you can't tell men from women here.
Unsexed in these catacombs we watch
for the asperges of the bath.
The damp walls bleed rice.
All dark, all si-
                    lent, we all pass.
We bow, each to each,
and some,
            not only young,
give the ancient kiss of peace,
standing in the alcoves again.
We reach for rain.
The Fall's spray touches each of us.
The glass
            over our eyes
                        weeps.
Cheeks
      are wet. Lips.
Even our teeth if our mouths gape.
We are caress-
                ed with wetness
all about our cloaks,
and we sway
            and float
broken out in a dark sweat,
complex, prodigious:
female, white, male, black, lay, religious.
At last we all
                peer out the stone holes
at the back of the falls

and see nothing but The Existential Wall:
water roaring out of the hidden hills.
Power passes us, detached,
                    abstract,
except for this cold steam
that licks and teases
                    until at last
we turn our drenched, glistening backs.

III

Aging, still
            agile
poet Eric Barker,
who has been coming
(I almost said springing)
back here
            for many years,
and I and two friends
strip at the still springs
with their
            full smell of sulphur—
here where bodies and warm water
are moon- and candle-lit, wind woven,
in a shallow cavern
                    open
to the heaving, iridescent sea
near
      Big Sur,

and we invade the great,
$$\text{Roman bath}$$
intimidat-
ing the Esalen teacher with his small class:
three naked girls in three corners of the big tub—
he, their leader,
$$\text{in the other.}$$
The candles waver
as the class takes cover
$$\text{and the mad teacher}$$
leaves with one student to find
a night watchman, leaving behind
the others:
$$\text{one of them}$$
already slithers
in a smaller tub with one of our friends.
The third girl now fully dressed—
and for the moment repress-
ed—stares
$$\text{at the rest of us}$$
lolling and floating our masculine flowers
as we give a naked reading of William Butler
Yeats to each other
$$\text{(taking care not}$$
to get the book wet)
and then we read to her
as she begins to listen.
$$\text{So she too strips and}$$
slips into the fourth corner,
becomes for a moment our teacher.

Her breasts come alive in the water.
Yeats
        will wait
and Keats—for Barker, with whom
we have been drinking wine
all afternoon
knows
        all the Odes
                by heart
as well as many
                bawdy songs:
"My long
        delayed erection,"
he'd recited, laughing,
"rises in the wrong direction."
But he too is silent
for the while, and
                sits stately,
buoyed by the
                water: its movement
makes his white
body hair seem to sprout.
Soon,
        we begin
                to say the poems again
and to touch each other—
                        the older
man, me,

the boys and the girl reading over the sea's
sounds
      by the candles'
light and the moon bright, burgeoning,
shin-
      ing time to time
                        as
the clouds pass.
                  In this gently flash-
ing light then
we all leave the tubs and run
dripping down the shore
together before
      any others come—
as hostile teacher, watchman.
But in that warm spring
water which we briefly left, everything
                              eventually heals:
for, by
      the sea
it flows out of these ancient, California hills,
which are the trans-
                  formed,
giant body of a once
powerful, feather, bone and turquoise-adorned
Indian Prince,
            and the sulphur is the changéd
sharp incense
            he burned daily as he chanted
year and year over for the sick young princess—

who took her loveliness
from the many-colored, fragrant trees
and the flickering sea.
Finally, unable to help,
                        he thought,
the tawny-skinned prince
died of his grief,
and his body became this mount-
ain. And everybody here who comes together
                                    in beli

is somehow bound, bathed,
                        and made
whole, e-
            ven as was she
by this gradual, glinting water,
the prince's continual tears for his sister.

So, when we return a little later
from our dance along the open shore
we find the Esalen
                    teacher there again,
and the watchman,
each with a woman.
They wait
            in that gentle, lunatic light for us.
They smile as they undress.
Eric Barker takes a leak,
begins reciting Keats,
and we all bathe and sing together
in the new waters of brother, sister.

JOHN LOGAN was born in Red Oak, Iowa, in 1923. He has degrees in biology and English and has done advanced work in philosophy. He is at present Professor of English at the State University of New York, Buffalo, and has taught at Notre Dame and San Francisco State. A critic and short story writer as well as a poet, he has been poetry editor of *The Critic* and *The Nation* and is co-editor of *Choice*, a magazine of poetry. This is his fifth collection of poems, the last being *The Zig Zag Walk*.